THE
PRINCESS
AND THE
FROG

Tiana's Dream

A STEPPING STONE BOOK™

Random House New York

CHAPTER 1

Do *you* believe that if you kiss a frog it will turn into a prince? I sure didn't. I thought kissing a frog would just be slimy and gross. Still, I am here to tell you that *sometimes*, if you try something new, you end up with a big, wonderful surprise—just like I did!

My name is Tiana. When I was a little girl, I loved fairy tales. I even believed in wishing on stars. Way back then, my mama was the best seamstress in the whole city of New Orleans. She still is, in fact. I used to ride the streetcar with her to work. Then, while she put the finishing touches on a dress or a suit, she would read me a story.

We often went to the mansion where my friend Charlotte LaBouff lived. Mama was always making big, fancy princess dresses for Charlotte. Lottie practically *was* a princess, with all her daddy's money. He loved to spoil his little girl.

Charlotte's favorite story was about the princess who kissed a frog and turned him into a handsome prince. Charlotte wanted to be a princess more than anything. She thought that wishing on the Evening Star would make all her dreams come true.

"I'd kiss a hundred frogs if I could marry a prince," she said.

"There is no way in this whole wide world I would ever, ever, ever, I mean *never* kiss a frog!" I told Charlotte. "Yuck!"

I had a very different dream from Charlotte's. It wasn't about princesses and frogs. It was about cooking delicious, wonderful food. I wanted to be a chef. My daddy and I were going to open our very own restaurant one day. We even had a place picked out—the old sugar mill down near the river. We were going to turn it into the fanciest restaurant ever! My daddy was already teaching me how to make the best food. He told my mama that I had a real gift for cooking.

One night, after making some gumbo, Daddy said, "A gift this special has just got to be shared." And so we had a really fun party to share our gumbo with all the neighbors. "Food brings folks together from all walks of life," Daddy always said. "It warms them right up and puts smiles on their faces."

Daddy and I knew that when we opened our restaurant, people would line up for miles just to get a taste.

Now, I cannot say that I completely disagreed with Charlotte's belief that wishing on the Evening Star made your dreams come true. I admit it: I wished, too.

I looked out my window that very night, filled with hope and wonder. I told Mama and Daddy what Charlotte had said to me. "If you make a wish on the Evening Star, it's sure to come true."

Mama assured me that it was okay. "Well, you wish on that star, sweetheart."

"But remember, Tiana, that old star can only take you part of the way," Daddy added. "You've got to help it along with some hard work of your own. And then you can do anything you set your mind to. Just promise your daddy one thing—that you'll never lose sight of what's really important."

I did just that. I wished on that Evening Star. And I worked hard—really hard. Before I knew it, fourteen years had gone by.

Daddy was no longer with us. But I remembered everything he had said about that restaurant. I was determined to make our dream come true. I had made a promise to him.

So every night, I waited tables at one restaurant, and every morning, I waited tables at another. Each day, I saved my tips in a coffee can in my dresser drawer. Sometimes I felt blue about how long it was taking those dimes and nickels to add up. But then

I'd tell myself, "Miss Tiana, every little penny counts."

I had a picture of a beautiful restaurant, just like the one Daddy and I had dreamed of owning. Daddy had written TIANA'S PLACE right on the front. He had given me the picture all those years ago. I carried it everywhere. That picture gave me hope that someday I was going to have a restaurant just like that one. But if anyone had told me exactly *how* I would have to get it, I would have said they were just plain crazy!

CHAPTER 2

The day my life changed forever started off just like any other. I put on my waitress uniform and rode the streetcar down to Duke's Diner. There were bands playing on the streets. Long lines of people were dancing along the sidewalk. But I didn't have time for singing and dancing. I needed to get to work!

So there I was, serving customers at Duke's. That was when Charlotte and her father, Big Daddy LaBouff, came in. Charlotte hadn't changed. Well, she was all grown up, like me. But she still dreamed about marrying a prince. And that day, she thought her dream was finally going to come true.

"Oh, Tia, Tia, Tia, did you hear the news?" She rushed over, waving the morning paper. "Prince Naveen of Maldonia is coming to New Orleans!"

Charlotte was all a twitter. Her family was hosting a masquerade ball that night. Big Daddy had invited Prince Naveen to be their special guest. Charlotte was sure this was her chance! She'd get Prince Naveen to marry her. Then she'd be a princess—just as she had always planned.

I gave Lottie a little advice: "My mama always said the quickest way to a man's heart is through his stomach."

Charlotte's eyes lit up. "Tia, you are a genius!" she exclaimed. She ordered as many of my man-catching beignets as I could make in time for her ball that night.

I was proud. I knew I made the best beignets in town. I made the dough myself and deep-fried it. When those little doughnuts were done, I just pulled them out and sprinkled them with sugar. Oh, they were good!

"Tonight my prince is finally coming, and I'm not letting him go," Charlotte vowed. She paid me well for all the beignets I was going to make. So well, in fact, that I finally had enough money to buy my restaurant—and I had earned every cent!

That afternoon, I met Mr. Fenner and Mr. Fenner. They were the two brothers who were selling that old, abandoned sugar mill Daddy and I had picked out all those years ago. They took my down payment and agreed to bring the paperwork to Charlotte's ball that very night.

I'll admit, the sugar mill was a mess. It had gotten much worse in the time since Daddy had first dreamed of fixing it up. Truthfully? It was about to fall down. The windows were broken. The walls were cracked. Pigeons roosted in the rafters. And about a hundred years of dust covered everything.

Mama surprised me by showing up at the mill with a very special gift—Daddy's old gumbo pot. I was so thrilled! She looked at me with a smile of support. I could tell that she was proud.

"It will all be worth it," I said. "A little bit of elbow grease—" Just then, a railing post fell over right next to us. "All right, *a lot* of elbow grease," I admitted, "and it will be the place Daddy and I always dreamed of."

Mama looked at me and said, "Tiana, your daddy may not have gotten the place he always wanted, but he had something better. He had love. And that's all I want for you, sweetheart."

All I knew was that I had a lot of work to do. But I didn't mind. I picked up a broom and started sweeping. In my imagination, I could see the crystal chandeliers twinkling. I could smell delicious food cooking. I could hear people laughing and talking. I thought things were finally going my way.

Well, guess what? I was wrong—as wrong as beignets without sugar or gumbo without hot sauce. And that is *very* wrong!

You see, somewhere else in town, trouble was brewing. The evil voodoo man, Dr. Facilier, was up to no good. He led Prince Naveen and his valet, Lawrence, into his dark lair. There were shelves full of jars of nasty-smelling powders, scary-looking dolls, and black candles. Strange masks were hanging on the walls.

It might sound fascinating, but it was just plain evil. Facilier was very good at tricking people. He made them believe that he would use his magic to make their greatest dreams come true. For example, Lawrence was a valet, but he dreamed of becoming royalty. Naveen had lost all his money when his parents cut him off, so he dreamed of being rich again. Facilier promised them both that he would make their dreams a reality. Soon Lawrence and Naveen were shaking Facilier's hands.

Suddenly, the arms of Naveen's chair turned into hissing snakes that locked him down. Facilier held a strange talisman that nipped at one of Naveen's fingers. Then the talisman turned red! Naveen and Lawrence were engulfed in swirls of dark smoke. Something very bad was happening. Then the room went dark.

CHAPTER 3

That night, the LaBouff mansion looked like an enchanted castle. Lanterns shone in the trees like pink and gold moons. Candles flickered on the tables. Music drifted through the air. As I set up my beignet stand, Charlotte swept over to say hello. She was dressed like a princess. But she was upset. Prince Naveen had not shown up yet. And Charlotte hated to be kept waiting.

"I never get anything I wish for!" she complained. "Maybe I've just got to wish harder!" She looked up at the Evening Star. "Please, please, please, please, please, *please*, please, please, please," she chanted.

I started to explain, "Lottie, you can't just wish on a star and expect—" Then we heard trumpets blaring.

Prince Naveen had finally arrived!

I watched the prince and Charlotte waltz across the dance floor as if they belonged together. I was happy for Lottie. Her dream was coming true. And so was mine. I was about to get my restaurant without help from any star.

But sometimes a dream is like a bubble, all light and shiny. Then someone comes along with a big old pin and—*POP!* Goodbye, dream.

Right then, Mr. Fenner and Mr. Fenner came up to the beignet stand. They were dressed as a horse. One Mr. Fenner was in the front of the costume. The other fit inside the rear end. They had bad news about my sugar mill.

"A fellow came in offering the full amount, in cash. Unless you can top his offer by Wednesday, you can kiss that place goodbye," said Mr. Fenner.

"But we had an agreement," I said. "You promised!"

I was so upset that when they started to walk away I grabbed the tail of their horse costume. I wanted to convince them to sell the sugar mill to me. But I guess I yanked that tail a little too hard. It ripped off in my hands, and I fell into the beignet stand. My costume was ruined.

Charlotte rushed to help me. She pulled me into her bedroom and gave me one of her princess dresses to wear. While I changed, she chattered about Prince Naveen. She was sure he'd ask her to marry him soon. Lottie was floating on air. And I was down in the dumps. Way, way down.

But Charlotte was so excited that she didn't notice. "Look at you!" she exclaimed when I emerged from behind her dressing screen. "Aren't you just as pretty as a magnolia in May!" She picked up a sparkling tiara from her dresser and placed it on my head. "It seems like only yesterday we were both little girls dreaming our fairy-tale dreams. And tonight they're finally coming true!" Charlotte rushed out of the room in sheer joy.

I was alone. I went out on the balcony and looked up at the Evening Star.

"I can't believe I'm doing this," I said to myself. I closed my eyes and wished. When I opened them, a big, green, slimy bullfrog was sitting on the railing.

He was staring at me. It was like a really bad joke.

"I reckon you want a kiss?" I asked the frog, not expecting an answer.

"Kissing would be nice, yes!" the frog replied.

He spoke! I shrieked and ran into Charlotte's bedroom. Frogs didn't talk. Frogs. Did. Not. Talk! Except this one did.

He followed me into the bedroom. "Please, allow me to introduce myself," he said. "I am Prince Naveen."

"But I didn't wish for a prince," I replied. I couldn't believe I was talking to a frog. I'd lost my restaurant. Was I losing my mind, too? Then I realized what the frog—er, prince—had just said.

"If you're the prince, then who is waltzing with

Lottie?" I asked. I was very confused.

The frog shook his head. "All I know is one minute I am a prince, charming and handsome, dancing away, and the next thing I know . . ." He hopped toward me. I picked up a book. I was ready to turn that frog into a green pancake.

"You must kiss me!" he exclaimed suddenly. I guess he thought that if I kissed him, he'd become human again.

He puckered his green, slimy lips. Yuck! "I'd really like to help you, but I just do not kiss frogs," I said. But he was one stubborn frog. I guess he had always gotten his way when he was a prince.

"Look. Besides being unbelievably handsome, I also happen to come from a fabulously wealthy family," he said. "Surely I could offer you some type of reward, a wish I could grant. Yes?"

I did feel sorry for him. And I wanted to help. Maybe I could turn him back into a prince—or whatever he was. Plus, I had worked so hard to get my restaurant. If I could manage just one very, very tiny kiss, maybe he could help me get the sugar mill back. I squeezed my eyes shut and leaned down. Yuck! I was kissing a *frog*!

Suddenly, something magical happened. There was a *poof*! Then I saw smoke. Everything seemed a little fuzzy.

When the smoke cleared, I looked at Prince Naveen. He was still small. He was still green. He hadn't changed. The kiss hadn't worked. Then I looked in the mirror. I screamed.

That frog had not been transformed into a human at all. But I had been transformed . . . into a frog!

CHAPTER 4

"**W**hat did you *do* to me?" I yelled at Naveen. I was so angry, I lunged at him and we tumbled through the open window. We landed on the drums in the band playing below.

Quickly, we dodged the drummer's drumsticks. I *was* a frog! And everyone at the ball wanted to catch us. Naveen and I ran. Well, we hopped, actually—but really, really fast!

We bounced off the drums. Then we slid down the back of Charlotte's dress. We hopped across the buffet tables and leaped over the punch bowls.

"Get them frogs!" Big Daddy LaBouff yelled. Of course, he didn't recognize me. But he acted as if he wanted to kill me! Finally, Naveen grabbed the strings of some balloons. We floated out of reach just in time.

The LaBouff mansion grew smaller and smaller as we floated higher and higher. At last it disappeared from sight. Slowly we drifted out toward the bayou. I had always loved the bayou. It was cool and green. At night, the stars sparkled on the water. But now, everything was so much bigger and scarier.

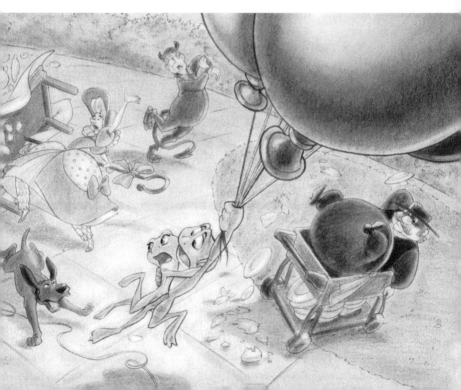

I couldn't believe this was happening to me. One minute I was planning my dream restaurant. The next I was a frog hanging on to another frog for dear life! To make things a whole lot more fun, it started to rain. Of course, frogs are supposed to like water. But not me.

This is what you get for kissing frogs, Tiana, I told myself.

As the balloons skimmed the bayou trees, Naveen explained to me how he had been turned into a frog by Dr. Facilier.

I couldn't believe it! This all happened because Naveen had been messing with Facilier and his voodoo. I could hardly stand to look at Naveen's frog face.

"It serves me right for wishing on stars," I said with a sigh. "The only way to get what you want in this world is through hard work."

"Hard work? Why would a princess need to work hard?" Naveen asked.

When I told him I was just a waitress dressed up

like a princess, he was absolutely furious.

"You lied to me! You never said you were a waitress!" exclaimed Naveen. "You—you were wearing a crown!"

"It was a costume party, you spoiled little rich boy!" I explained.

He said the kiss hadn't worked because I wasn't a real princess. He tried to blame me!

Then he confessed something. "I am completely broke! Ha ha!" He had no money. His parents—the King and Queen—had cut him off. Could things get any worse?

Oh, yeah. You bet your beignets they could!

Right then, the balloons popped. Down we went into the muddy bayou. We came up covered with gunk.

"You said you were fabulously wealthy!" I yelled. Naveen screamed as a giant leech crawled up his arm. I quickly flicked it off.

"You're broke, and you had the gall to call me a liar?" I said, fuming.

But before we could continue our argument, a catfish leaped out of the water and snatched the leech. Naveen and I both screamed.

"It was not a lie! I fully intend—" Naveen leaned against a branch to catch his breath. But the branch was really the leg of a giant bird! I yanked Naveen out of the way a split second before the bird swooped down with its big beak. We ran. Again.

"I fully intend to be rich again once I marry Miss Charlotte LaBouff," Naveen said, panting. "If she will have me."

"You're a prince?" I asked, just to make sure he wasn't lying again.

"Obviously!" he replied.

"She'll have you," I said. We slid down a tree trunk and flew through the air. Luckily, we landed on a log in the water.

Then I looked Naveen straight in his bulging eyes. "All right, then, once you two are married, you are going to keep your promise and get me my restaurant, right?"

"I made that promise to a beautiful princess, not a cranky waitr—" Just then, Naveen saw something moving through the water toward us—alligators! Our "log" was an alligator, too! We dove off and paddled to a hollow tree. I climbed inside. But Naveen was still in the water.

"Help me get out of this swamp, and once I marry Charlotte, I shall get you your restaurant," he promised. I couldn't just leave him there, even though I wanted to. So I lowered a vine and he crawled up beside me. We were safe . . . for now.

Meanwhile, back in New Orleans, Facilier was working his evil magic. When Facilier had turned Naveen into a frog, he had also made Lawrence look exactly like Naveen! Facilier had a plan: Using his magic talisman, he would keep Lawrence disguised as Prince Naveen and have *him* marry Charlotte. And once that happened, Facilier would control the prince's valet *and* the LaBouff family fortune.

But Facilier needed Naveen to keep the magic working in that talisman. Without the magic, Lawrence would no longer look like the prince. So Facilier was searching for Naveen. The evil doctor called upon the shadows from dark, dark places. He told the shadows of the power they would all share as soon as he was the richest man in New Orleans. Then he convinced them to hunt down Naveen and bring the frog to him.

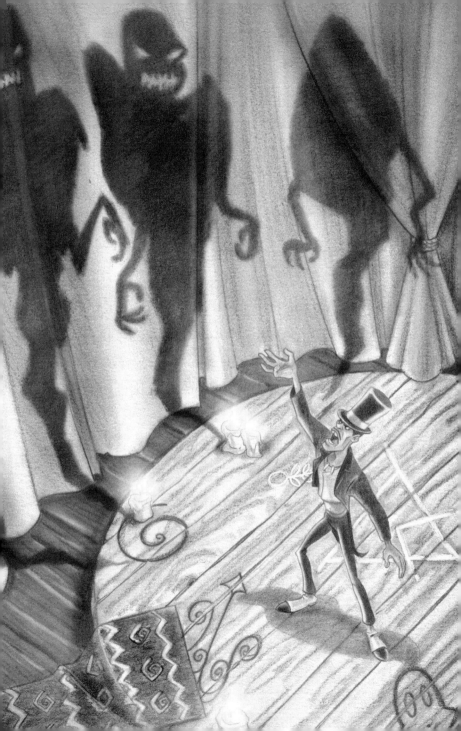

CHAPTER 5

I woke up the next morning at the crack of dawn and got right to work building a boat. We needed to get back to New Orleans and find a way to become humans again. While I worked, His Royal Frog Highness slept late.

"Rise and shine!" I yelled to him as soon as the boat was finished. Naveen came out of the hollow tree trunk and lazily climbed into my boat. Of course, he let *me* do all the work. I struggled to paddle through the bayou while Naveen lounged in the back, strumming on a little ukulele he had made.

Suddenly, I saw a huge alligator mouth rising from the water!

"I know that tune!" the alligator said. I had been expecting to see a large set of teeth coming toward me and then to take a slippery slide down the alligator's throat. But it turned out that he was just excited by the music Naveen was playing.

The alligator pulled a trumpet out of the water and began tooting a sweet jazz tune.

"Play it, brother!" Naveen exclaimed. Then he joined in with his ukulele.

Before long, the two of them were talking about music as if they'd known each other forever. I don't think I'd ever seen such a happy alligator. Of course, I'd never met an alligator at all—especially not a trumpet-playing one. His name was Louis, and he loved jazz. (He adored his trumpet so much that he had named it—er, her—Giselle.) Louis's big dream was to play his music on the riverboats. But he had tried once, and everybody on the boat had chased him away. He had been too scared to try again. Ever.

"Whenever people see me coming, they run away," Louis said. "But now I have friends I can talk jazz with all day long!"

Well, playing around was *not* going to get us out of the mess we were in. I was determined to find a way out of the bayou and get someone to turn us back into humans.

"Thank you kindly for not eating us, but we'd best be on our way," I told Louis. When we said we were really humans, he just laughed. But then I

explained about Dr. Facilier, the voodoo man. Louis stopped laughing. "Voodoo? Like the kind Mama Odie does?" he asked.

Louis said Mama Odie was an old woman who lived in the bayou. She knew all kinds of spells. She knew how to break them, too. We asked Louis to take us to Mama Odie's, but he refused.

"Through the deepest, darkest part of the bayou? Facing razor-sharp pricker bushes and trappers and hunters with guns? No," he said nervously.

Then Naveen surprised me by being clever. "If only you were smaller and less toothy, you could play jazz to adoring crowds without scaring them," he said to Louis.

That gave Louis an idea. He agreed to take us to see Mama Odie. And he would ask her to turn him human, too.

Maybe Naveen isn't such a silly, careless frog—er, prince—after all, I thought. We climbed onto Louis and he swam off. The alligator blew his trumpet and sang about the music he would play when he became human. Naveen played along. The sun was warm. The sky was clear. We were on our way to being human again. I felt fine—for a frog.

Everything would have been nearly perfect if I had been human and if Naveen had been a little less annoying. I had never met anyone who could only think about one thing: having fun! It seemed like Naveen had never worked in all his life. Can you imagine? Well, I had a feeling all of that would change soon. Getting out of the bayou was definitely going to be hard work!

CHAPTER 6

Naveen and I both relaxed as we took the free ride atop Louis. But at least *I* was trying to think of a plan. We needed to find Mama Odie. We would have to convince her to make us human again. Then Naveen would marry Charlotte, and I'd get my restaurant. It would be as easy as baking biscuits.

We traveled all day. I was getting hungry. Suddenly, a fly buzzed by.

"What? Oh, no . . . no, no, no," I said, shaking my head. There was no way I was going to eat a bug! But I couldn't stop myself. Something inside me just wanted that bug!

Snap! Naveen's tongue darted out at the fly. *Snap!* My tongue shot out, too. And our two tongues crashed into each other, becoming hopelessly entangled. Oh, this was not good! Louis tried to help, but he just made things worse. Naveen and I were tied together in a knot. Never had I imagined that I would one day get all tangled up with a prince. But there I was! And I was completely speechless . . . or, er . . . tongue-tied.

Luckily, the fly we had tried to catch buzzed over to us. He was actually a friendly little firefly named Ray. Soon he managed to find exactly the right spot to tug. Within seconds, Naveen and I were untangled. Thank goodness!

Ray offered to show us the way to Mama Odie's place. Louis had tried to lead us, but he was not very good with directions. Ray whistled, and hundreds of twinkling fireflies formed a sparkling chain of light in the evening sky.

"Keep the line flowing and the lights glowing!" Ray called to his family. We followed the glimmering lights through the mist. Ray was determined to light up the bayou and show us the way to Mama Odie.

Finally, we were close. Ray told his family they could leave. He would take us the rest of the way himself.

"Adieu, ma famille!" Ray called to them as they left. "Oh, and don't forget to tell Angela that Ray-Ray says *bonne chance!*"

"Is that your girl, Ray?" I asked.

"Nah," he replied. "She's my uncle's neighbor's cousin twice removed. So you know we're tight. But my girl is Evangeline."

"Evangeline?" I asked.

"She's the prettiest firefly that ever did glow!" Ray said with an extra sparkle. "You know, I talk to Evangeline most every night. She's kind of shy and doesn't say much. But I know in my heart that someday we are going to be together."

"That's so sweet," I said.

"Just do not settle down so quickly, my friend," said Naveen. "There are plenty of fireflies in the swamp."

I guess Naveen thought he was giving Ray helpful advice. But I could tell that Ray had already found his one and only true love.

As we made our way to land, I tried to clear a path through some thornbushes. That's when I heard Louis shriek. "Pricker bushes got me! Gator down! Gator down!"

Ray stepped in and started pulling the thorns out of Louis. The journey to Mama Odie was taking longer than I thought. I was anxious to undo the spell and I still had my dream! Even if Naveen just felt like having fun for the rest of his life, I would keep working toward my goal. I was going to sit in my restaurant someday soon and watch people enjoying my food. *That* would be my fun!

CHAPTER 7

Suddenly—*whump!* A net swooped down and caught Naveen. Three frog hunters had spotted us! Another hunter tried to grab me, but I got away.

As soon as Louis saw the hunters, he hid. But not Ray. That brave little firefly flew up one hunter's nose. The startled hunter dropped the net holding Naveen, and the prince hopped out.

Just then, the second hunter tried to hit me with a club. He slipped, and I thought I might get away. But he toppled over a log and flipped me into a cage. I was trapped!

Thankfully, Naveen came back to save me. I couldn't believe it! He jumped into the boat. Then he hopped onto the head of one of the hunters, whose name was Reggie. As Naveen kept hopping around, Reggie's two silly sons began hitting him over the head, trying to get Naveen. Reggie got banged up, but Naveen didn't get hurt—or caught. In all the chaos, I managed to escape. Then Naveen and I started hopping back and forth. We tricked the hunters into hitting one another. At last, all three of them lay in a pile at the bottom of the boat.

"These aren't like any frogs I ever saw!" Reggie moaned. "They're smart."

I admit that I was feeling pretty proud of myself and Naveen. Of course, it felt even better to see those scared hunters run away from us as soon as they could.

Naveen and I looked at each other and smiled. We were actually starting to warm up to one another. Then Louis interrupted us with a groan. He was still covered in thorns. Ray started to pick them out of Louis's sore skin. Since we would clearly have to wait awhile, I offered to cook dinner. And I decided I would put Naveen to work.

"Mince the mushrooms," I told him. I gave him a makeshift knife. But Naveen had no idea what to do. So I taught him—*chop, chop, chop.* He seemed impressed—and determined to finish cutting the rest of the mushrooms by himself.

"You know," he said, "I have never done anything like this before." He sighed deeply. "When you live in a castle, everything is done for you all the time. They dress you. They feed you, drive you, brush your teeth."

"Oh, poor baby," I said, trying not to giggle at the thought of Naveen having to live such a pampered life.

Then Naveen said something else. "I admit, it was a charmed life, until the day my parents cut me off, and suddenly I realized I don't know how to do anything."

"Well, hey, you have the makings of a decent mushroom mincer," I teased. Actually, I was feeling a little sorry for him. He really didn't know how to do anything. He was totally lost!

Soon we were laughing and joking like good friends. After we ate, we sat by the fire Ray had built. We felt full and happy. Ray had taken all the prickers out of Louis. I could tell that Naveen was proud he had helped with dinner.

Suddenly, Ray pointed to a shining light in the sky. "There she is," he said softly. "The sweetest firefly in all creation."

That's when we realized that the love-struck firefly's sweetheart, Evangeline, was actually the Evening Star!

As Ray started singing to Evangeline, Louis played his trumpet softly.

Naveen asked me to dance.

"Oh, no. I don't dance," I replied.

But he insisted. "If I can mince, you can dance." I couldn't believe I agreed to it. We started to move to the music. It was kind of nice. We gazed into each other's eyes. Naveen leaned in close. I suddenly got butterflies in my stomach! It was a magical moment. We were just about to kiss when I opened my eyes and backed away. *I can't do this*, I thought. I couldn't kiss Naveen. He was supposed to marry Lottie. It was her dream to marry a prince. And anyway, I always said that I would never, ever, ever kiss a frog. I had done it once and look where that had gotten me.

"Lottie's getting herself one heck of a dance partner," I said. "We, um—we'd best be pushing on." We had Mama Odie to find and an evil spell to break.

CHAPTER 8

As we made our way to find Mama Odie, dark shadows suddenly loomed over Naveen. One of them grabbed him and pulled him through the swamp. I tried to hold on to his arms, but the shadows were too strong. Louis and Ray came to help, too. We all tried to pull Naveen back.

Then—*FOOOMM!* Blinding flashes of light destroyed the shadows. It seemed that light was the only defense against the dark creatures. We were terrified and relieved at the same time. Who— or what—was helping us?

We turned and saw the biggest, most frightening shadow approaching. We were all ready to run.

Suddenly, a small, wrinkled old woman came out from behind a tree! She held a smoking gourd in her hands. A large snake was draped around her shoulders like a scarf.

"Not bad for a hundred-and-ninety-seven-year-old blind lady. Which one of you naughty children has been messing with the voodoo man?" Mama Odie asked. She knew that Facilier had sent those horrible shadows.

Mama Odie led us into her home, which was an old shrimp boat stuck in a tree. We didn't have to tell her why we had come. She already knew what we wanted—to become human again. But then she asked a very odd question. "Have you figured out what you need?"

We told her that we needed to be human. Naveen needed to marry Charlotte. I needed my restaurant. Mama Odie just shook her head. "Y'all don't have the sense you were born with!" she shouted. "Y'all *want* to be human, but you're blind to what you *need*!"

Though Mama Odie herself was blind, she seemed to look right into my eyes. She told me that my daddy was a family man. She certainly knew a lot about me, even though we had never met before! There was something special about her. She knew that my daddy had taught me well. He always knew what was important. I just had to think harder about what I really needed.

So I tried to think, but I could only come up with one answer. "I need to work even harder to get my restaurant," I said. Mama Odie just sighed. Then she stirred her tub of gumbo.

I peered over her shoulder and looked into the gumbo. I saw a magical image of Lottie and Big Daddy LaBouff in her bedroom. He told her that he was going to be the king of Mardi Gras, the biggest celebration in New Orleans. That would make Charlotte the princess of Mardi Gras. But Charlotte would only be the princess until Mardi Gras was over.

"You only have until midnight to get that

princess to kiss you," Mama Odie said to Naveen. "Once she does—boom!—you'll both turn human!"

"What about me, Mama Odie?" Louis asked. "I want to be human, too!" He was still dreaming of playing music on those riverboats.

Mama Odie laughed. "Jabber Jaws, you'll find everything you need." Then she turned to all of us. "Come on, now! There's a lot of river between here and New Orleans. You best get to swimming!"

But Louis had an even better idea. He led us directly toward some pink and purple lights gleaming on the river. A big steamboat was chugging by. On board, people in costumes were dancing to a jazz band. That was it! We'd hitch a ride on the steamboat. Next stop: New Orleans!

CHAPTER 9

We climbed on board the steamboat and looked around. Suddenly, we heard people heading our way. We quickly found hiding places—except for poor Louis. He was just too big! A group of musicians went up to him. They were all wearing animal costumes.

"Man, that is one killer-diller costume!" said the bandleader.

Louis's eyes lit up. The band members thought he was a jazz musician in an alligator costume!

"We're playing at Mardi Gras. Come join us!" said the band.

Louis was thrilled. This was his big chance!

He joined the musicians and went off to play jazz in a real band.

"We can't miss this! Little Louis is going to finally play with the big boys!" said Ray.

Ray and I followed Louis, but Naveen chose to stay behind.

"I'll catch up with you later," he said.

Naveen was acting strange. I wondered what he was up to.

Later that evening, Naveen found me and led me to a quiet little table with candles and flowers. He had even prepared a romantic dinner of fruit he had minced himself.

"I just wanted to show you a little something to celebrate our last night together as frogs," he said with a grin.

I gasped. It was all so lovely! "All my years, no one's ever done anything like this for me," I said.

We looked into each other's eyes. For a moment, I felt something I'd never expected to feel.

The ship's horn blew. Naveen and I watched the

lights of New Orleans reflected in the water. I looked across the river. There it was—the old sugar mill! I pointed it out to Naveen. Then I told him about my dream to turn it into a restaurant.

"I know it may not look like much now," I said, "but when I'm done, it's going to be the toast of New Orleans: folks lined up as far as the eye can see just to get a taste of our food. . . ."

"*Our* food?" Naveen asked.

"Oh, no. My daddy," I tried to explain to Naveen. "It was his dream to turn that old sugar mill into the finest restaurant east of the Mississippi. Tomorrow, with your help, his dream is finally coming true."

"Tomorrow?" Naveen asked.

"If I don't deliver that money first thing tomorrow, I lose this place forever."

Naveen lowered his head. "I see. Tiana, I love . . . the way you light up when you talk about your dream. A dream that is so beautiful that I promise to do whatever it takes to make it come true."

As the ship turned toward the docks, Naveen went off to find Ray and Louis. I stood on the steamboat alone. Suddenly, I felt very confused. I looked up at the Evening Star and spoke to her. "Evangeline, I've always been so sure of what I wanted. . . ." I paused for a moment. "What do I do? Please tell me." Evangeline twinkled back at me.

At that very moment, on the other side of the boat, the evil shadows struck again. They grabbed Naveen and carried him away. None of us heard his screams for help. All we knew was that we couldn't find him anywhere on the boat. And it was time to head out to the Mardi Gras parade. We only had until midnight to break the spell.

CHAPTER 10

Ray, Louis, and I finally made it to New Orleans. Mardi Gras was already in full swing. It was one big party. There were floats, people in costume, balloons, confetti, and jazz music everywhere.

I thought Naveen might be waiting for us, but he was nowhere to be found. I was beginning to get worried. I asked Ray if he knew anything. That romantic little firefly couldn't help himself. He told me that Naveen wasn't going to marry Charlotte. "He's in love with *you!*" he blurted out. "And as soon as he gets himself kissed, he's going to find some whole other way to get you that restaurant." Ray paused. "Uh-oh. I said too much."

"You said just enough, Ray!" I cried, filled with joy. Naveen was in love with me! I suddenly realized that I loved him, too. I had to find him!

"Keep your eyes out for the biggest, gaudiest float with a Mardi Gras princess about to kiss herself a frog!" I told Ray. Float after float went by. Then I saw the one I was looking for. I stopped, frozen in my tracks. I felt colder than ice cream on a winter day.

Charlotte was dressed in a princess wedding gown. She stood on top of a giant wedding cake. Beside her was the very handsome Prince Naveen. And he was *human* again! A minister was reading the wedding vows. The human Naveen was smiling tenderly at Charlotte.

"That can't be right!" Ray exclaimed. "You're still a frog! Mama Odie said . . ."

I didn't wait to hear the rest. My heart was breaking. My dreams were crumbling. I hopped away as fast as I could. I thought Naveen did not love me. I was going to remain a frog forever.

Ray followed. He found me in the cemetery, sitting near a tombstone. "I know what we saw with our eyes," he said. "But if we just go back there, we're going to find out your fairy tale has come true."

I shook my head. I just couldn't hope anymore. I was done dreaming and wishing. I had learned my lesson. "Just because you wish for something doesn't make it true!" I snapped.

"But . . ." Ray paused. "It's like my Evangeline always says to me—"

And then, without thinking, I blurted out something I would later regret. "Evangeline is nothing but a star," I told Ray. "A big ball of hot air a million miles from here. Open your eyes now, before you get hurt."

Ray's lips trembled. His eyes filled with tears. But he knew I was speaking from my own broken heart. He forgave me. And he refused to give up.

"Come on, Evangeline," he said softly. "We're going to show her the truth."

Then he flew away. And I was alone.

CHAPTER 11

As soon as Ray reached Charlotte's float, he buzzed around until he heard the real Naveen. The prince was still a frog. And he was locked in a small chest!

You see, when the shadows had taken Naveen from the boat, they had delivered him to Dr. Facilier. The wicked man grabbed Naveen and used him to refill the magic in the nasty talisman. Instantly, Lawrence turned back into the spitting image of Prince Naveen. That's when Facilier locked the real Naveen in a chest. And Lawrence took his place to marry Charlotte!

Ray squeezed through the lock and opened the

chest. The second he was free, the frog Naveen leaped on Lawrence, making him lose his balance.

Lawrence and Naveen tumbled onto the street. Lawrence grabbed Naveen and ran into a big cathedral. Facilier stormed in after them.

"Get back up on that wedding cake and finish this deal!" he yelled at Lawrence.

But Naveen shot his frog tongue out. He grabbed the talisman from Lawrence. With a scream, the valet changed back into himself. Facilier lunged for the talisman, but Naveen tossed it to Ray.

The talisman was so heavy that the little firefly could barely carry it. Still, he managed to fly off with it through the crowd. Instantly, the evil shadows appeared and chased after him.

Meanwhile, Louis was getting ready to play with the same band he had performed with on the steamboat. As he was about to climb aboard a float, he saw Ray struggling with the talisman. Louis looked at Giselle, his trumpet. Then he looked back

at Ray. He had no choice. He had to help his firefly friend.

Ray flew as fast as he could. Louis followed far behind. The brave little firefly found me again. I was still sitting in the cemetery, alone and feeling sorry for myself. Ray handed me the talisman. He told me to take it and run. And that's exactly what I did. I hopped away as fast as I could, with Facilier's own shadow chasing me. Ray stayed behind to fend off the other shadows with his light. But Facilier showed up and swatted Ray to the ground. And then Facilier stepped on him!

Meanwhile, I kept on hopping with that talisman—until Facilier and the shadows caught up with me.

"Back off, or I'll break this thing into a million pieces!" I threatened. I held the talisman high up in the air.

The shadows stopped. Facilier approached. He held his hands out for the talisman—as if I were about to let him put his cold claws on it. No way was that going to happen! But the evil Dr. Facilier had more tricks up his sleeve.

He suddenly blew some sparkling dust at me. Everything turned cloudy, and moments later I found myself standing in my dream restaurant. The tables were set with silver and crystal and china. I looked at my hands. I was human again!

"Now, isn't this a whole lot better than hopping around the bayou for the rest of your life?" Facilier said. "All you've got to do to make this a reality is hand over that little old talisman of mine."

"No, this isn't right," I said nervously.

"And don't forget your poor daddy. That was one hardworking man," Facilier said as he created another illusion.

I couldn't believe it. I could see Daddy on the back porch at home. It was the first time I had seen him in so many years. He was greeting the neighbors with a big pot of gumbo. His smile was so warm and loving. I missed him very much.

Then Facilier interrupted my vision. "You can

give your poor daddy everything he ever wanted."

As I looked at my daddy, I really did want to give him everything he ever wanted. But seeing him made me remember his most important message to me. And then suddenly it all became crystal clear.

"My daddy never got what he wanted," I said firmly. "But he had what he *needed*. He had love. He never lost sight of what was really important. *And neither will I!*" I raised the talisman and smashed it to the ground. The illusion instantly vanished. I was a frog again.

Facilier looked at the broken talisman. Boy, was he angry! But he was also scared. He screamed out as the dark shadows swooped down upon him. Soon the only thing left of Dr. Facilier was his top hat.

Without wasting another second, I hopped back to the parade. I needed to find Naveen!

CHAPTER 12

I raced back to the cathedral in time to see the police take Lawrence away. Charlotte and Naveen were on the front steps.

"This is so much to absorb," Charlotte was saying to Naveen. "Let me see if I got this right. If I kiss you before midnight, you and Tiana will turn human again? And then we are going to get married and live happily ever after, the end?"

"More or less," Naveen said. "But remember, you must give Tiana all the money she requires for her restaurant. *Because Tiana—she is my Evangeline.*"

"Wait!" I called out. Both Charlotte and

Naveen were surprised to see me. "My dream wouldn't be complete without you in it," I told Naveen. I would rather be a frog with him than a human separated from him forever.

Charlotte blinked. "All my life, I read about true love in fairy tales," she said, sniffling, "and now, here it is right in front of me. Tia, honey, you found it!" She turned to Naveen. "I'll kiss you, Your Highness. No marriage required!"

But it was too late. The clock had struck midnight. Charlotte kissed Naveen anyway. Nothing happened. He was still a frog. So was I. But the important thing was that we were together.

Suddenly, Louis ran up. He was in tears. He opened his palm and there lay little Ray. His tiny firefly light was barely glowing. "The voodoo man has laid poor Ray low," Louis said.

Naveen and I rushed over. Ray had been hurt badly. But he also looked calm and peaceful. He smiled when he saw that Naveen and I were holding hands.

"We're staying frogs, Ray," I told him.

"And we're staying together," Naveen added.

Ray smiled, happy. "I like that very much. Evangeline likes that, too," he said. Then his light flickered out for the last time.

Filled with grief, we took Ray home to the bayou. Naveen, Louis, and I watched Ray's family put him on a leaf boat in the water. Louis played a slow, sad song on his trumpet. The boat

floated away, disappearing into the mist.

For a moment, the clouds cleared. I looked at the sky. I saw the Evening Star shining brightly. *Evangeline*, I thought. Then I looked again. A new star shimmered right beside her. Ray was with his Evangeline. Now they shone side by side, just the way Ray had always believed they would. Love always finds a way.

CHAPTER 13

The next morning, Naveen and I stood together before Mama Odie.

"I now pronounce you frog and wife!" the old woman exclaimed. "Now give your lovely bride some sugar!"

Naveen kissed me. Suddenly, swirls of magical sparkling dust surrounded us.

"Ooh! This is going to be good!" I heard Mama Odie say. When I could see again, I looked at Naveen. He was tall. He was handsome. He was human! And so was I.

"Kissing a princess breaks the spell!" Mama Odie laughed. Then we understood! When Naveen married me, I officially became a princess.

"You just kissed yourself a princess!" I cried.

"I'm about to do it again!" Naveen replied.

Everyone cheered.

Soon Naveen and I returned to New Orleans for our royal wedding. My mama was there, and she had made me the most beautiful wedding dress ever. Naveen's parents, the King and Queen of Maldonia, came, too!

Shortly after that, Naveen and I bought the sugar mill and worked hard to fix it up—together. When we opened our restaurant, we were both proud. It was a jumping, jiving jazz supper club. The music was the hottest in town—with Louis as the star trumpet player. But, as Daddy had always said, it was the food that brought people together.

I hadn't just gotten what I wanted. Naveen and I had also found what we *needed*—each other.

So now you know how my dream came true. And if I have any advice, it's this: Dream. Wish. Work hard. But along the way, don't ever forget what's really important—love, family, and friends— just like Daddy said.